Table of Contents

Cast of

ME

CLAUDIA
That's me. I'm thirteen, and I'm in the seventh grade at Pine Tree Middle School. I live with my mom, my dad, and my brother, Jimmy. I have one cat, Ping-Ping. I like music, baseball, and hanging out with my friends.

MOM

MOM is Laura's aunt, and Aunt Inez's sister. She and I are going to Aunt Inez's house early so that we can spend some time with Aunt Inez and Laura before the big day.

LAURA

LAURA is the bride! She's also my oldest (and favorite) cousin. Laura has always been someone I look up to. She's pretty, smart, funny, and a great cousin!

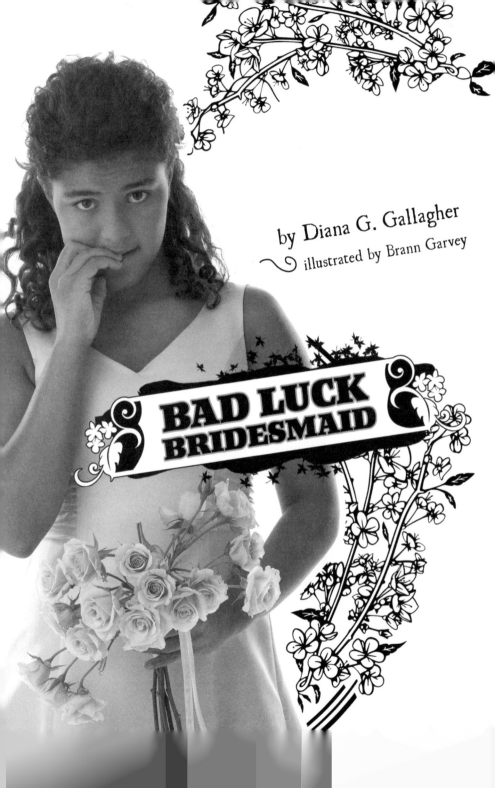

by Diana G. Gallagher

illustrated by Brann Garvey

BAD LUCK BRIDESMAID

Claudia Cristina Cortez is published by Stone Arch Books
151 Good Counsel Drive, P.O. Box 669
Mankato, Minnesota 56002
www.stonearchbooks.com

Library of Congress Cataloging-in-Publication Data
Gallagher, Diana G.
  Bad luck bridesmaid / by Diana G. Gallagher ; illustrated by Brann Garvey.
    p. cm. — (Claudia Cristina Cortez)
  ISBN 978-1-4342-1573-4
  [1. Weddings—Fiction. 2. Hispanic Americans—Fiction.] I. Garvey, Brann,
ill. II. Title.
  PZ7.G13543Bad 2010
  [Fic]—dc22
                              2009002544

Summary: Claudia has been asked to be a bridesmaid in her cousin Laura's
wedding. Claudia's excited, so she finds lots of information about weddings online.
Soon she knows all about wedding traditions and luck. But when she arrives at
Laura's house, everything starts going wrong. Is Claudia the bad luck charm?

Creative Director: Heather Kindseth
Graphic Designer: Carla Zetina-Yglesias

Photo Credits
Delaney Photography, cover

Printed in the United States of America

Characters

AUNT INEZ is Laura's mom, my mom's sister, and my aunt. She makes really delicious meals — I think she's the best cook I know!

SALLY is Laura's best friend. She'll be the maid of honor in Laura's wedding. She's also Joey's aunt. Sally and Laura have known each other since before they were my age!

PABLO is Laura's fiance. They met in college, when Pablo asked Laura if she could help him with his French paper. Laura said yes, and before long, they were dating. Now they're getting married!

Cast of

JOEY is Sally's six-year-old nephew. He's going to be the ring bearer in Laura and Pablo's wedding.

JOEY

UNCLE JORGE is Aunt Inez's husband and Laura's dad. He'll be walking Laura down the aisle on the big day.

UNCLE JORGE

DAD isn't crazy about weddings, but he really loves Laura, so he's excited to come to hers. He and Jimmy will drive to the wedding together on the day of the wedding.

DAD

Characters

JIMMY is my sixteen-year-old big brother. He loves music, computer games, and ignoring me as much as possible.

JIMMY

GRANDMA VARGAS

GRANDMA VARGAS is Laura's grandma, but not mine (she's Uncle Jorge's mom).

MARTIN is Pablo's fourteen-year-old cousin. He's a groomsman in the wedding.

MARTIN

CHAPTER 1

GUESTS, GIFTS, AND GOWNS

Invited, Excited

I love a lot of things about my life.

Some of the things I love:

- How the kitchen smells when Mom cooks breakfast

- Hearing my dad laugh (because he's so serious most of the time)

- Dressing up in weird costumes on Halloween

- My three best friends: Monica, Becca, and Adam

- Chocolate cream pie

- Red nail polish

- My Silver Jet rollerblades

- My cousin, Laura

This weekend is Laura's wedding. And I'm going to be in it!

Claudia Cristina Cortez = junior bridesmaid

* * *

Laura's family only lives an hour away, but the drive to their house seemed ENDLESS.

"How much longer?" I asked. Mom and I were staying at my aunt and uncle's house for the wedding. Aunt Inez is Laura's mother. She's also my mother's older sister.

"Twenty minutes," Mom said.

"Too long," I said. My stomach rumbled. **"I'm starving."**

"I'm sure Aunt Inez will have something ready for lunch," Mom said.

I was counting on it. Aunt Inez loves to cook. My brother, Jimmy, can eat a whole pan of her custard flan dessert by himself. In sixty seconds flat!

I took the wedding invitation out of my bag. A thin piece of see-through paper covered the gold lettering. The inside of the envelope was gold, too. The invitation had come with a small R.S.V.P. card.

R.S.V.P. =

French: Répondez s'il vous plaît =

English: Reply, if you please.

Mom had already sent the little card back to let Laura know our family would attend.

Jimmy and my dad weren't coming until the rehearsal dinner on Friday night. They don't like all the *getting-ready fuss.* They just like the parts with food.

𝔽◉◉𝔻! My stomach growled again. Thinking about the wedding took my mind off soup, salad, and sandwiches.

The night before we left for Aunt Inez's house, I was so **excited** about being a bridesmaid that I couldn't sleep. So I looked up weddings online. Our modern traditions began in some very strange ways. There are dozens of superstitions about weddings, and most of them are about **bad luck.**

I don't believe in superstitions. Still, I brought a new penny for Laura to put in her shoe.

It probably won't make the bride and groom healthy and rich, but it can't hurt.

Better safe than sorry.

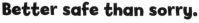

Busy Bride

Laura is twelve years older than me, but we're as close as sisters. I hadn't seen her in weeks. I was so excited!

As soon as we got to her house, I burst through the front door shouting, "Laura! We're here!"

"Is that you, Mildred?" Laura yelled. She ran down the stairs.

"No, it's me," I said, smiling. I opened my arms for a hug.

"Oh. Hi, Claudia," Laura said. She sounded **disappointed**. She didn't hug me. She looked at her watch.

Aunt Inez came in from the kitchen and hugged my mom. Then she hugged me.

"Who's Mildred?" I asked.

"The dressmaker," Laura said. She looked
out the window and added, "She's LATE."

"I'm sure she'll be here soon," Aunt Inez said.
"Let's have lunch while we're waiting."

"I can't eat," Laura said. "I have to finish the
seating chart for the rehearsal dinner. Where is it?"

"On the coffee table," Aunt Inez said.

"I'm **glad** you're here, Aunt Perla," Laura said to
my mom.

She looked out the window again. Then she hurried
out of the room.

I felt like I was invisible.

Mom and I sat down at the kitchen table.
Aunt Inez served us tiny tuna sandwiches,
potato salad, and sweet pickles.

"The crusts are cut off the sandwiches!" I
exclaimed. "I love these."

"I know," Aunt Inez said. "I made them just for
you."

I ate two sandwiches. Then I asked, "Is Laura mad at me?"

"My goodness, no!" Aunt Inez said. She laughed. "She's just nervous about the wedding."

"**Brides want everything to be perfect,**" Mom explained.

"And nothing ever is," Aunt Inez said. She sighed. "We almost didn't have a wedding cake!"

Mom looked shocked. "Why not?" she asked.

"We ordered the cake six months ago," Aunt Inez said. "Two weeks ago, I called to check on the order. The bakery had new owners, and they'd LOST our order!"

"That's bad," I said. Wedding cakes are a big deal. They have lots of layers and fancy icing decorations. And they're expensive, and they take a really long time to make.

"At least you had time to fix it," Mom said.

Aunt Inez nodded. "Yes, but Laura still thinks something else will go *terribly wrong*," she said.

Just then, the doorbell rang. Laura ran downstairs and opened the door. A man handed her a package.

Laura carried the box into the dining room. She put it on the dining room table.

I ran into the dining room and slipped on a throw rug. I didn't fall down. I fell against the table. It was piled high with Laura's wedding gifts.

A box fell off the pile.

"**Look out!**" Laura squealed.

I caught the box before it hit the floor. "Got it!" I said. I put the box back on the table.

"**You've got to be more careful, Claudia,**" Laura snapped.

Her angry tone startled me. Laura had never yelled at me.

I could tell that she felt 🅑🅐🅓 about it right away. "I'm sorry, Claudia," Laura said. "I didn't mean it."

"That's okay," I said. I was about to ask if she'd take a break for lunch with us, but then the doorbell rang again.

Laura ran to get it. I just stood in the dining room **alone**.

Dress Fitting

The person at the door was Mildred, Laura's dressmaker. Suddenly, **everyone** had something to do.

Laura and Mildred went upstairs to make sure the wedding dress fit.

Aunt Inez made salads and finger food snacks for the reception.

Mom called the florist, the organist, and the bakery.

Nobody needed my help, so I watched TV.

Some people say that a wedding is the **biggest** event of a woman's life. I think winning an Olympic gold medal or being elected President of the United States might be **bigger**.

I don't really want to get married. Mom thinks I'll change my mind.

I don't.

"Time for your fitting, Claudia," Aunt Inez said after I'd been watching TV for a while.

I turned off the TV and ran upstairs. I couldn't wait to see my bridesmaid's dress. And maybe now Laura had **some time to spend with me.**

I stopped in the bedroom doorway. Laura was wearing a long white gown. The white veil on her head trailed all the way down to the floor.

"You look **beautiful**," I whispered.

Laura beamed with delight. "Thanks, Claudia," she said.

"Do the shoes fit?" Mildred asked. "You'll have to be comfortable in them for hours!"

"No **pinched toes**," Laura told us. She lifted her skirt to show me the shoes. "And there's room for a good luck penny."

"I brought you a shiny new one," I said.

"Fantastic! **That was nice of you**," Laura said. She looked pleased.

Then I remembered something I read online. "It's **bad luck** to wear your whole bridal outfit before the wedding," I blurted out.

Laura gasped. "Is that true, Mildred?" she asked nervously.

Mildred shrugged. "It's just a superstition," she said. **"Don't worry about it."**

"Why didn't you tell me?" Laura asked. She looked really worried. I thought she might start to cry. "I knew something would go wrong. *I just knew it.*"

I felt awful. I didn't know Laura would be so upset. Then I remembered another custom.

"Are you wearing something *borrowed*?" I asked.

"No," Laura said nervously.

"Then you're not wearing your entire bridal outfit!" I exclaimed. "So no bad luck."

"You're right!" Laura said. She smiled. "What a RELIEF."

Mildred helped Laura carefully take off her dress and veil.

Then it was my turn. The dressmaker slipped a long gown over my head.

I gasped when I looked in the mirror. I did not beam with delight.

I like comfort more than **style**. I love red and despise pink, and I had never worn anything that looked like ruffled curtains.

Until I put on my bridesmaid dress.

The dress was pink, but I only had to wear it once, so that was okay. The straps and the big bow in back weren't my style, but they were okay too. But I hated the gigantic flower on the front.

"What do you think, Claudia?" Laura asked. "Isn't it gorgeous?"

"I don't like the flower," I said. It was too big, too bright, and it bounced when I moved.

I looked in the mirror again. Then I looked at Laura and Mildred. "Are all the bridesmaid dresses the same?" I asked.

"Yes," Mildred said.

"We'll look like a **cartoon garden**," I said.

"You'll look fine," Laura said.

Then Sally, her best friend, walked in.

Laura hugged Sally. "I can't **wait** to show you my honeymoon wardrobe!" she said, pulling Sally out of the room.

I could hear them giggling from down the hall. I had to finish my fitting.

I stood still while Mildred pinned up the hem of my dress. It was hard to stand completely still, but listening to Laura and Sally giggling through the wall was harder.

They were best friends. Sally was the maid of honor. I knew I shouldn't be upset, but Laura was ignoring me.

My feelings were hurt.

I told myself to get over it.

Bridal Note

Make a list of each wedding gift and who sent it. Write thank-you notes by hand and mention the gift. The notes should be mailed no later than three weeks after the wedding.

CHAPTER 2

BRIDAL SHOWER
Getting Lost

The maid of honor holds a bridal shower for the bride. This usually happens weeks before the wedding. Sally decided to wait until the last minute. That was a great idea.

1. Out-of-town relatives and friends could come.

2. Laura would get more presents.

Aunt Inez and Laura drove to Sally's house with the two other bridesmaids. Mom and I brought **Mrs. Garcia**, the mother of Laura's fiancé, Pablo.

"Do you have the directions?" Mom asked me.

"Yep," I said. I held up the paper I'd written the directions on. Aunt Inez had talked **too fast** when she told me how to get to Sally's, and my writing was *scribbled*. I could read most of it, though.

"After you back out of the driveway, go left at the street," I told my mom.

"I hope it's not far," Mrs. Garcia said. **"I get carsick."**

"Open the window," I suggested.

"What's our next turn?" Mom asked.

"Go right at the light on Blueberry Street," I told her. I looked out the window and read the street signs. We passed five traffic lights before Mom pulled over.

"Did you write the directions correctly?" Mom asked.

"I'm pretty sure," I said. I squinted at the paper. I couldn't read the first two words. "Okay, **I'm not sure**," I admitted.

"Are we lost?" Mrs. Garcia asked.

"I'm afraid so," Mom said.

Mom called Sally. She quickly figured out my mistake.

"We should have turned right at the driveway," Mom said, "and then left at the first street." She turned the car around.

"I'm sorry I messed up," I said.

"It's not a big deal," Mom told me. "We'll only be about twenty minutes late."

"I *hate* being late," **Mrs. Garcia** said.

I hoped Laura wouldn't be mad.

Play to Win

The other guests were waiting when we walked into Sally's house. "It's **my fault** we're late," I confessed.

"That's okay. You're here now," Laura said. She led Mrs. Garcia to a comfy chair and sat down beside her.

Laura was **ignoring** me again, but she wasn't mad. And I wasn't upset. A bride has to be **extra nice** to her future mother-in-law.

Mom and I put our present on the gift table. Then we sat on folding chairs by Aunt Inez.

When everyone was sitting down, Sally gave each person *a ribbon with a bell* on it. We all tied them around our necks.

"What's this for?" a bridesmaid asked.

"Everyone has to say '**bride**' or '**groom**,' not **Laura** and **Pablo**," Sally said. "If you goof, the person who notices it gets your necklace. Whoever ends up with the most necklaces wins a prize."

I love games, and I always play to win.

Sally passed out pads and pencils for the first game. "Okay, Laura, go into the kitchen," she said.

I called out, "You didn't say '**bride!**'"

Sally **slapped her forehead** and gave me her necklace. Then she took Laura into the kitchen.

Laura came back wearing an apron. The apron had kitchen utensils and gadgets attached to it.

"Study the things on the apron," Sally told us. "You have two minutes." She set a timer.

"Turn around, Laura," Aunt Inez said. "I can't see the apron."

I waited a second. When no one else spoke up, I did.

"**You said her name,** Aunt Inez!" I told her.

Aunt Inez gave me her necklace. Then we all tried to remember everything that was on Laura's apron.

I knew the names of **most of the things,** but there were one or two I didn't recognize. I tried to remember as many things as I could.

When the timer rang, Laura took off the apron.

"Now you have five minutes to write down the things that were on the apron," Sally said.

"Does Laura get to **keep** the kitchen stuff?" another bridesmaid asked.

I waited again. No one else caught the mistake, and I got another necklace. **That made four.**

"Claudia is very good at this game," Mrs. Garcia said.

I have a good memory, too, but I didn't want to hog the prizes. I only wrote down half the things I remembered seeing on Laura's apron.

One of the bridesmaids won a $20.00 gift card to a movie theater. Laura got to keep the apron and utensils.

"You'll need them in your new house, Laura!" Mrs. Garcia exclaimed.

"Bell, please!" I said, smiling. Mrs. Garcia handed me her necklace.

Sally glanced at Laura.

"I think that's long enough to play the bell game!" Sally said, smiling. "Claudia is our winner, with five bells!"

The prize was a cookbook. I tried not to look **disappointed**.

Mom says I'll have to learn to cook someday. I don't think so. **I can survive on sandwiches and cereal.**

Sally handed Laura a closed pink parasol. "Putting gifts in a parasol started in the late 1800s," she told us.

Laura opened the parasol. A bunch of fancy beauty products fell out.

"That's why this is called a **bridal shower**," Sally said. "The bride is **showered** with gifts."

"I didn't know that," my mom said. "That's a COOL tradition."

"Isn't it bad luck to open an umbrella inside?" I asked.

Laura dropped the parasol. "More bad luck? Oh, great! Now my wedding really is JINXED!" she said nervously.

Sometimes my mouth is quicker than my brain. I forgot that Laura is **superstitious**. I scrambled to fix the problem.

"Your wedding isn't jinxed," I said quickly. "I wasn't thinking. Umbrellas keep rain off. Parasols are used on sunny days for shade. They aren't the same thing."

"Claudia is right," Aunt Inez said. "Opening a parasol in the house isn't bad luck."

"Oh, good," Laura said. "I can't handle any bad luck before the wedding!"

I knew I had to watch what I said from now on. If something went wrong with the wedding, **Laura might think I was the jinx!**

Present Time

It was time for Laura to open her gifts.

As she sat down to open all the presents, I remembered another thing I'd read on the Internet.

"I read online that the first gift you open at your shower is the **first gift** you'll use after the wedding," I told her.

"Oh, cool!" Laura said. "I can't wait to see what it is."

Sally took a gift off the pile. It was from Mom and me.

"Open something else first, Laura," I said. I knew what our present was. Laura wouldn't want to open it first.

Laura *ignored* me. She ripped open the wrapping paper.

"What is it?" Sally asked.

"If Claudia's superstition is right, it could be a DISASTER," Laura said. She looked worried. "It's a tool set. Why would I need a hammer and a hacksaw right after the wedding?"

"To **fix** something," Sally said.

"Or to **break** something," Mrs. Garcia suggested.

"That's why we got you tools," I explained. "You never know when you'll need them."

"I keep mine in a kitchen drawer," Mom added. The tool kit also had three screwdrivers, a pair of pliers, and a metal tape measure.

Laura's next present was a silver picture frame. The third box held two sets of His and Her towels.

"Thank you, Grandma Vargas," Laura said.

"Grandma Vargas? **No way!**" I exclaimed.

"What is it, Claudia?" Mom asked.

"Whoever gives the third gift will have a **baby**," I said.

"That's **ridiculous**," Laura said, laughing. "Grandma Vargas is *not* going to have a baby."

"I know," I said. "That proves it. **Superstitions are just silly fun.**"

Bridal Note

Long ago, fathers gave their daughters' husbands money and gifts when they were married. This was called a dowry. However, if a father didn't like the groom, he didn't give anything. When this happened, the bride's friends gave her presents instead. American brides began having showers for fun in the 1890s.

CHAPTER 3

WEDDING WARNINGS
The Ring Bearer

Sally came to Laura's house the next morning. She brought doughnuts and her six-year-old nephew, Joey.

I poured a glass of O.J. and opened the doughnut box.

"I get the chocolate one!" Joey yelled. He grabbed the doughnut and bumped my arm. Juice splashed up my nose.

"Why is he here?" I asked.

"Joey is the ring bearer," Sally explained.

"He has to practice with the ring pillow," Laura said.

That was a **relief**. I was sure they were going to make me babysit. I always get stuck babysitting. "Don't let the rings fall, Joey," I told the little boy. "Or Laura and Pablo's marriage will be DOOMED."

Laura gasped.

Sally groaned.

Joey shrugged, quickly finished his doughnut, and ran out of the kitchen.

Laura looked frantic. "*Are you trying to spoil my wedding*, Claudia?" she asked.

"Of course not," I said, frowning. I knew Laura was nervous, but her question wasn't fair. *It hurt my feelings.*

"Joey doesn't want to carry the ring pillow," Laura said.

"He thinks he'll **mess up**," Sally explained.

"We told him the wedding will be fun," Laura added, "but he's still **nervous** about it."

Joey didn't look nervous to me. He was throwing the ring pillow down the hall like a Frisbee.

Sometimes I wish I didn't talk so much.

If I hadn't told Joey not to drop the rings, **everything would be fine.**

But I did tell him. So one of two things would happen.

1. Joey wouldn't drop the rings, and everything would still be fine.

2. Joey would drop the rings, and Laura would blame me if her marriage went kablooey.

There was only one thing I could do. I had to help Joey practice so he wouldn't drop the pillow!

Luckily, I'd brought a bunch of my own jewelry along because I didn't know what Laura would want me to wear in the wedding. We didn't have the real wedding rings, so I put two of my rings on the ring pillow.

Joey marched back and forth in the hall, balancing the rings on the pillow. When he wanted to quit, I promised him another doughnut, cartoons, and a **dollar**. He practiced for half an hour before he got **bored**.

"Can I be done now?" Joey pleaded. "The rings didn't fall off once."

The rings couldn't fall off. They were tied with a ribbon.

The ribbon was sewn onto the pillow. But **I didn't tell Joey that.**

"Okay, you can be done," I said. "I'm glad you didn't drop the pillow."

Aunt Inez asked me to go to the store with her. Joey was gone when we got back.

I went upstairs to see Laura and Sally. They weren't 𝕄𝔸𝔻 at me anymore.

"Thanks for helping Joey," Laura said, smiling at me.

"He took the pillow home to practice some more," Sally added. "You're **really good with kids.** Joey won't do anything when I ask."

I spent a lot of time babysitting. I had one rule for kid control: **Give them something they wanted so they'd do what I wanted.** Works every time.

"What are you two doing?" I asked.

"Packing everything I need at the church," Laura said.

"We need the new penny you brought,"
Sally said.

I took the penny out of my pocket and gave it
to Laura.

A penny was one of the things a bride always wore
at a wedding.

Something old, something new,

Something borrowed, something blue,

And a penny in her shoe.

Everybody knew the old poem. I knew what each
thing meant.

Old links the bride to her family.

New brings good fortune.

Borrowed keeps loved ones nearby.

Blue means love and loyalty.

The penny promises health and wealth.

"Do you have the other things in the poem?" I
asked. "Something old, something new, something
borrowed, and something blue?"

"My wedding dress is NEW," Laura said. "And my garter is **blue**."

I knew that brides wear elastic garters on their legs. In the old days, garters used to hold up stockings. Now brides just wear them for fun.

"I **borrowed** Sally's perfume," Laura went on. "And my great grandmother's gold bracelet is very, very **old**."

"Can I see it?" I asked.

"Sure," Laura said. She looked in her jewelry box. Then she frowned. "The bracelet isn't here," she said nervously.

"Did you already pack it?" I asked.

Sally looked in the suitcase. "It's not in here," she said.

We searched the bedroom. Sally shook out the sheets and blankets. Laura went through every drawer in her dresser. I even crawled under the bed with a flashlight.

The bracelet was gone.

"Can you wear something else that's old instead?" I asked.

"Yes," Laura said, "but the bracelet belonged to Great Grandmother. It was the new thing at her wedding. It was the old thing that my grandmother and mother wore."

"It's a **family tradition**," Sally said.

"Not anymore. I lost the bracelet," Laura said. She sniffled back a tear. "Maybe my marriage really is DOOMED."

Time Trouble

Laura, Sally, Aunt Inez, Mom, and I searched the whole house. We didn't find the bracelet. After we'd looked for more than an hour, we all met in the kitchen.

Laura looked really sad.

"Sometimes things turn up where you've already looked," Aunt Inez said.

"That happens to me with **socks and pencils**," I said.

"I'm sure we'll find Great Grandma's bracelet," Aunt Inez said.

"Before the wedding starts at two o'clock tomorrow?" Laura asked.

Another alarm went off in my head. "Uh-oh," I said quietly.

Laura sighed. "Now what?" she asked.

"Nothing," I said, shaking my head. "Just something else I read online." I did not want to point out another **bad luck wedding myth.**

"Come on, Claudia," Sally said. "What is it?"

"You have to tell," Laura insisted.

I sighed. Then I pointed to the clock on the kitchen wall. "If the wedding starts at 2 o'clock, the big minute hand is on the 12," I said.

Everyone nodded.

"During the wedding, the big hand moves from 12 down to 6," I said. "So the ceremony is the high point of the marriage. And everything goes DOWNHILL from there."

"Things get *worse*," Laura said. She sat down.

"But if the wedding starts at 2:30," I said, "the minute hand moves from 6 up to 12. So the marriage will get better and better."

"We can't change the time now," Aunt Inez said. "The invitations say two o'clock."

"It's just a **stupid superstition** anyway," Sally said.

"I guess," Laura said. I could tell that the superstition bothered her. And that bothered me.

I had to stop being a **bad luck blabbermouth**. Or Laura might be sorry she asked me to be her junior bridesmaid.

Bridal Note

According to another superstition, there are good days and bad days to have a wedding: Monday for health, Tuesday for wealth, Wednesday best of all. Thursday for losses, Friday for crosses, Saturday for no luck at all.

CHAPTER 4

LAST-MINUTE FRENZY
More Problems

We ate lunch. Then Aunt Inez looked at Laura. "Take a nap," Aunt Inez said. "You'll feel better."

"I can't sleep," Laura said. She rested her chin on her hands. "What if we **NEVER** find Great Grandma's bracelet?"

Then I had an **idea**. I ran into the living room to get a deck of cards.

Whenever I visited Laura, we always stayed up late. We talked, laughed, watched movies, read magazines, and gave each other beauty treatments. Sometimes we played cards. A game might help her relax.

I ran back into the kitchen just as Laura left with Sally. "Where're they going?" I asked.

"To get their nails done," Mom explained.

"A **best friend** has the best chance of making bad things better," Aunt Inez said.

I understood that. **My problems didn't seem so awful when my best friends tried to help.**

Aunt Inez left. She had to go to the bakery to make sure the wedding cake was ready.

Mom left too. "I'm taking Laura's dress to the dry cleaner," Mom said.

"Why?" I asked. "Laura didn't wear it long enough to get it dirty."

"The wrinkles have to be steamed out," Mom explained.

After Mom left, I played solitaire. No packages came, but the D.J. called. I wrote down the message.

Meet D.J. 1:30 at reception hall so he can set up.

Mom got back first and read my note. "We can't send someone at 1:30," she said. "The wedding starts at 2. Nobody wants to **miss** the wedding ceremony."

"Jimmy won't care if he misses it," I said.

The phone rang again, and Mom answered it. She listened to the person on the other end.

Then she said, "Oh no! I'll be right there."

"Who was that?" I asked when she hung up.

"The dry cleaner," Mom said. "I dropped the dress off **too late**. It won't be done until 3 o'clock tomorrow."

"But the wedding starts at 2 o'clock!" I exclaimed.

"We can have the dress in the morning, but I have to go to the dry cleaner's now and pay extra," Mom explained. She paused before she left. "**Don't tell** Aunt Inez or Laura about the D.J. or the dress."

I promised. Both problems were solved. My aunt and cousin didn't need to know.

Still, just for a minute, **I thought the bad luck superstitions were real.**

The Rehearsal

Laura was still upset about the bracelet when she and Sally got back from the nail salon. She was also worried about her hair and her nail polish and a dozen other little things.

Mom said all brides worry. But brides in medieval times had a lot more to worry about.

Sometimes knights from other kingdoms kidnapped them! A girl's family had to use tricks to keep her safe. Some of the tricks became modern traditions.

The tricks:

1. Other women dressed up in fancy dresses too.

2. They stood with the bride during the ceremony.

3. The bride only came to the real wedding, not the rehearsal.

The reasons:

1. Bad knights couldn't tell who was getting married.

2. Then they didn't know which woman to kidnap.

3. Until after the wedding, when it was too late.

The traditions:

1. Brides invite other women to be bridesmaids.

2. It's bad luck for the bride to practice the ceremony.

3. Another woman pretends to be the bride at the rehearsal.

Aunt Inez picked me to be the pretend bride at the rehearsal that night. "Just walk naturally," she said. "Don't rush."

Uncle Jorge and I stood together at the back of the church.

"Are you ready?" Laura's father asked me.

"I guess so, Uncle Jorge," I said.

I held his arm and took a deep breath. The organist played, and we walked.

My hands were sweaty. **My legs felt like noodles,** and I started shaking.

Halfway down the aisle I **stumbled**. Uncle Jorge caught me, and I didn't fall.

I had to stand with Pablo at the altar. That was **embarrassing**. He smiled and winked so I'd relax.

Instead, I burst out laughing. The organist shushed me.

"Sorry," I mumbled.

I looked up at the ceiling. I looked down at my feet. I counted the colors in the stained glass window. I did not look at the groom again.

Joey twirled the ring pillow. Then he sat on it.

Everyone else tried not to look bored.

When we were done, Sally took me aside. "Be careful tomorrow, Claudia," she said. "If a bridesmaid stumbles walking down the aisle, she'll be an old maid."

"Oh, thanks," I said.

I wasn't worried. I'm not superstitious.

I also have an **Exciting Things To Do When I Grow Up** list.

1. Write a bestselling novel.

2. Canoe in Alaska.

3. Attend the World Series when my favorite team plays.

Getting married isn't on it.

Still, I didn't want to fall over during the wedding. It would ruin Laura's wedding video. And then everyone would watch **Claudia the Klutz** over and over again for the rest of my life!

Rehearsal Dinner

After the rehearsal, we went to Pablo's **favorite** restaurant. Mr. and Mrs. Garcia rented a private party room for the rehearsal dinner. Everyone in the wedding party, plus all of the family members, would be going to the dinner.

When we arrived, Laura was smiling and relaxed.

So was I. There weren't any superstitions about rehearsal dinners.

It was also my **last chance** to hang out with my favorite cousin. **Laura wouldn't have time for me after she was married.**

I started to walk over, but just then, Dad and Jimmy came in.

"When do we eat?" Jimmy asked.

Mom pointed at a table with trays of crackers, cheese, and dip. **Jimmy** nodded and headed over to the table right away.

My brother's list of favorite things is very short: *his computer, his bass guitar, and food.*

"Are you having fun getting ready for the wedding?" **Dad** asked.

Several answers went through my mind.

A. True: "Not really."

B. Sort of true: "My dress fits."

C. False: "It's been a blast!"

I picked C. I didn't want to answer any more questions.

Luckily, Dad didn't ask me anything else. He left to talk to Mom.

By then, Laura and Pablo were surrounded by other guests. I couldn't SQUEEZE through the crowd. If I wanted time with my cousin, I'd have to sit by her at dinner.

But Laura had made a seating chart for the dinner. There were name cards at every seat. Sally was sitting next to Laura. I picked up her card and went to find mine.

Mom caught me. She made me put Sally's card back. She said I had to sit in my assigned spot because that's the way Laura wanted it.

I ended up sitting between Joey and Pablo's aunt Matty. She snorted when she chewed, and her flowery perfume made me SNEEZE.

We were in the middle of dinner when Laura clinked her fork against her glass.

"Pablo and I have special thank-you gifts for our wedding party," she said, smiling. "We are so glad to have such **wonderful people** in our wedding."

Pablo gave his groomsmen engraved pen and pencil sets. He gave Joey a gift certificate for the pizza arcade.

"**Cool!**" Joey exclaimed. "I'm going to take my whole class!"

Laura gave Sally and the rest of us bridesmaids engraved silver candy dishes. They said:

With affection and gratitude,

Laura and Pablo

The dish was beautiful, but **I was disappointed**. I thought Laura would give me something special. I was her favorite cousin.

Of course, that was before I started telling her about **superstitions that made her feel bad** all the time.

Pablo raised his glass to toast the bride. "To Laura, the love of my life," he said, smiling.

Then Laura toasted Pablo. "To my handsome husband-to-be," she said. "I am so lucky to have a person like you in my life."

Joey dropped a dinner roll in my lap. I stood up to shake off the crumbs.

Uncle Jorge saw me standing. "It looks like Claudia wants to give the next toast," he said.

I swallowed hard. Everyone watched me.

"Well, uh, I want to say . . ." I began.

My throat closed up, and my mouth
went dry. *I was totally tongue-tied.*

Everyone was staring at me. They all expected me
to say something!

"To Laura," I said. "Don't worry about all that bad
luck stuff because **superstitions are stupid** and nobody
really believes they come true. Well, not very often
anyway, and it's probably just **coincidence** when they
do, so—"

Joey stood up. "Claudia said you guys are
doomed!" he yelled.

Everybody gasped.

I wished I could shrivel up and disappear.
Instead, I sat down and hid my red face.

**I wouldn't be surprised if Laura never spoke to me
again.**

Bridal Note

The rehearsal dinner gives family and friends a chance to relax and get to know each other. Out-of-town guests are often invited too. Traditionally, the groom's parents usually plan the dinner.

CHAPTER 5

CEREMONY COUNTDOWN
Seven Years

Some people get mad and stay mad. **Not Laura.** She was glad to see me on Saturday morning.

"I'm so excited! I want everyone else to be happy, too. **I'm getting married today!**" she said happily when I walked downstairs.

We squealed and hugged and jumped up and down. Then we ate breakfast together.

After breakfast, Sally arrived at Laura's house. "Let's go!" she said.

"Bye," I told Laura. "See you at the church!"

"Don't be SILLY," Laura said, smiling at me. "You're coming with me and Sally. It **wouldn't be as fun without you.** Let's go get ready!"

At the church, Laura had her own room to get ready in.

The bridesmaids shared a big dressing room. Our dresses were hung on a bar. A stylist tied flowers and ribbons in my long hair. Sally did my makeup.

After Sally was done, I picked up a mirror to look at my face. But my hands were sweaty, and the mirror slipped.

It fell onto the floor and cracked into a hundred little pieces.

"Oh no!" I said. I bent down to carefully pick up the pieces of the mirror.

"Don't let Laura see that," Sally told me. "She'll worry about the bad luck."

I shook my head sadly. "If you break a mirror, it's seven years of bad luck," I said. "But it's not bad luck for Laura's wedding. **It's bad luck for me!**"

"I thought you didn't believe in that stuff," Sally said.

"You're right, I don't," I told her. But **secretly**, I was a little *worried*.

"Now the dress!" Sally said.

She slipped the dress over my head. She was careful not to mess up my hair. She fastened the big bow in back.

I stared in the mirror on the wall. All I could see was the big, ugly flower. "I HATE that flower," I said.

"So do I!" Sally admitted. She made a face.

The other bridesmaids hated the flowers too.

"Let's take them off!" I said.

"Okay," Sally said.

She carefully snipped the stitches that held the flowers in place. We hid the flowers behind a chair. My pink dress was still too **frilly**, but it looked better.

Then Joey charged into our dressing room.

"You look **adorable** in your tuxedo," Sally said.

"It's itchy!" Joey said, pulling at his collar.

Sally tucked in Joey's shirt tag and patted his lumpy pocket. The lump didn't go away.

She reached in and pulled out the missing bracelet.

I gasped. The bracelet hadn't disappeared after all!
Joey had taken it.

"Why did you take Laura's bracelet, Joey?" Sally asked.

"Claudia took the rings away," Joey said. "And I had to practice."

"We thought the bracelet was lost," I said.

"It wasn't lost," Joey replied. "It was just in my pocket."

"Where's the ring pillow?" I asked.

"I gave it to Laura's dad," Joey said. "Pablo isn't here yet."

I looked at the time. It was 1:37. Pablo was supposed to be at the church by 1.

The groom was late.

Better or Worse

Laura **freaked out** when Sally told her that Pablo was late.

"Pablo isn't here? Where is he?" Laura asked.

"We don't know," Sally said. "We haven't heard from him."

"What if he changed his mind?" Laura asked. "What if he was in an **accident?**"

"Somebody would have told us," Sally said. "I'm sure he's fine."

"Then why hasn't he called?" Laura wailed. **"This is a nightmare!"**

"Don't cry, Laura," Aunt Inez said. "You'll smudge your makeup."

My mom's cell phone rang. "It's Jimmy," she said.

Oh no, I thought.

Jimmy was supposed to meet the D.J. That meant **something had gone wrong.** Otherwise, Jimmy wouldn't be calling.

I followed Mom into the hall. She talked to Jimmy for a little while.

After she hung up, I asked, "What's happening?"

"The D.J. is 𝕊𝕀𝕮𝕂. He sent a replacement," Mom whispered.

"Is that bad?" I asked.

Mom nodded. "This one is really *rude*," she said. "He's not dressed nicely, and he said he won't play the songs Laura wants."

I knew that wasn't the worst thing that could happen. After all, we wouldn't need a D.J. if Pablo didn't show up.

No groom, no wedding, no reception.

Grandma's Baby

Mom and Sally went to find Pablo's parents and ask if they'd heard from their son.

Sally came back with Laura's grandma. "You're not going to believe this!" Sally said.

"Did you hear from Pablo?" Laura asked.

"No, but your grandmother has some **exciting** news," Sally told her.

Grandma Vargas looked happy. "The bridal shower myth about giving the third gift came true! I have a baby!" she told us.

Everyone was SHOCKED. "What do you mean, Grandma?" Laura asked.

"My friends gave him to me yesterday," Grandma Vargas said. She opened her purse. A tiny Chihuahua stuck his head out.

Just then, Mom rushed back in. **"Pablo's here!"** she announced. She was laughing really hard.

"Oh, thank goodness! Why was he so late?" Laura asked.

Mom paused to stop laughing. "His tuxedo pants only came to his knees!" she said. "They were hemmed up for a **shorter man** to wear. The tailor forgot to fix them. Pablo's neighbor came over and took the hems down."

"Thank goodness!" Laura said. She laughed, but then she gasped. "What time is it?"

Sally looked at her watch. "2:23," she said.

"Everybody's waiting. What will we tell them?" Laura asked. She looked frantic. **"Nothing is going right,"** she said sadly.

"Everything is going right," I said. "Even this delay is **good luck**!"

"It is?" Laura asked, puzzled.

"It will be 2:30 when the wedding starts," I pointed out. "The big hand will be going up during the ceremony! **Everything that happens after that will be better!**"

Bridal Note

Brides haven't always worn white dresses. In 1840, England's Queen Victoria wanted white lace sewn into her wedding dress. She began the popular custom of wearing white. Since white dresses were hard to clean back then, most wedding dresses were only worn once. Being married in a special white dress became a tradition.

CHAPTER 6

I DO AND DON'TS

When everyone was dressed, Aunt Inez handed us our bouquets.

The bouquets were made of white and pink flowers with wisps of green fern. The bride's bouquet was bigger and had white ribbons. The bridesmaids had pink ribbons.

I wasn't **NERVOUS** until we lined up in the back of the church. I was going to be the first one to walk down the aisle!

The Wedding Procession
Bridesmaids

Maid of Honor

Ring Bearer

Bride

Being first wasn't all bad. I had the best view of the church while we waited.

The guests of the **bride** sat on one side of the church. The groom's guests sat on the other side.

An usher walked Aunt Inez down the aisle. She sat in the front row on the left. Laura's family and friends sat on the left side, too.

Another usher escorted Mr. and Mrs. Garcia. They sat in the front row on the right side of the church.

A side door opened up front, and the minister entered. The best man and groomsmen lined up on the right. **Pablo** waited in the center at the very front of the church.

"Don't tip the pillow, Joey," Sally whispered.

"I won't," Joey insisted.

The organist began to play.

Everyone turned to look down the aisle.

"Off you go, Claudia," Sally said.

My feet felt like anchors! I couldn't move.

"Claudia!" Sally whispered. "Move!"

I moved.

I walked slowly, with a fake smile frozen on my face. I stared at the minister's feet.

I didn't want to laugh if Pablo winked. Somehow, I reached the front of the church without stumbling or giggling.

Joey stopped three times coming down the aisle. He scratched his leg, he scratched his head, and he rubbed his nose on his sleeve. But he didn't tip the pillow.

"Pablo!" Joey exclaimed. **"I didn't drop the rings."** Everyone in the church laughed.

"Great job!" Pablo said, smiling.

Then the organist started to play the Wedding March. All of the guests stood up and turned toward the back of the church.

Laura and Uncle Jorge walked slowly down the aisle. Laura looked so beautiful in her long white dress and veil. **My eyes filled with tears.**

I didn't have a tissue.

I blinked and sniffed them back.

Laura and Uncle Jorge stopped at the front of the church. Then Uncle Jorge joined Aunt Inez.

My nose started to **itch**, but everyone was looking at me, so I couldn't scratch it. **I twitched and wiggled my nose, but it still itched.**

The minister talked about **love, respect, and patience.** He said those things would make Laura and Pablo happy. I wasn't happy. **The itch was driving me crazy!**

"Do you, Pablo Garcia, take Laura Vargas to be your wedded wife?" the minister asked.

"I do," Pablo said.

I pretended to sniff my bouquet. I rubbed my nose on a flower stem. The itch stopped, but then I had to **SNEEZE!** I scrunched my nose again to hold it in.

Joey rubbed his nose. This time, the ring pillow tipped. The ribbon wasn't tied tightly, and the rings began to slide off.

Luckily, the best man caught the rings before they fell.

The minister recited the wedding vows, and Laura repeated them.

She promised to love Pablo:

1. for better or worse

2. for richer or poorer

3. in sickness and in health.

Pablo put Laura's ring on her finger. "This ring is a symbol of my love," he said.

I wiggled my nose so I wouldn't sneeze. And I wiggled my toes so I wouldn't **faint**.

Laura gave Pablo his ring. "This ring is a symbol of my love," she said.

"I now pronounce you husband and wife," the minister said. "You may kiss the bride."

Pablo kissed Laura.

I sneezed.

The bride and groom went back up the aisle as **everyone clapped.**

Then the bridesmaids and groomsmen followed them out.

"When can I take off my suit?" Joey asked when we got outside. **"I'm hot."**

"After we're done taking pictures," Sally said.

"I don't want my picture taken," Joey announced.

"It won't take long," Sally explained. "Laura and Pablo just want a few shots of the whole wedding party."

"I'm not having fun," Joey said. He scowled and folded his arms.

I knew how he felt. I couldn't wait until the pictures were over and we could go to the reception.

Soon, the guests left for the reception. The wedding party went to the garden behind the church. The photographer took photos of different groups.

1. everyone

2. the groom and groomsmen

3. the bride and bridesmaids

We cheered when the photographer finished. Everyone was hungry. Joey led the frilly dress and tuxedo STAMPEDE to the parking lot.

Then we heard a shout.

"Help!"

It was the minister. "I locked my keys in my car," he said.

"If I had some tools, I could help you out," Pablo said.

"I have tools in my car!" Laura exclaimed. "Claudia and Aunt Perla gave them to me at the bridal shower."

"The first gift superstition said you'd need them," I said. "And now you do!"

"Isn't that **amazing**?" Aunt Inez asked. "You were right, Claudia!"

Pablo used Laura's hacksaw blade to pop the lock in the minister's car.

Then the bride and groom rode to the reception in a limo.

Mom and I drove Laura's car.

Laura's friends had decorated her car. They painted **"Just Married"** on the window. A dozen cans and shoes were tied to the back. The cans clanked. Other drivers honked at us. *Mom and I laughed so hard we cried.* It was a very weird and noisy drive.

Bridal Note

In medieval times, the bride and groom's families sat on opposite sides of the church so they wouldn't fight. That's because the families often didn't like each other. The groom stood on the right so he could reach his sword to protect his bride. That's why at some modern weddings, the bride's guests sit on one side, and the groom's guests sit on the other.

CHAPTER 7

HAPPILY EVER AFTER
Memories

When we got to the reception, we found out that Laura had **fired** the D.J. because he wouldn't play her songs. Luckily, she had rented the equipment from a different company.

"I've got everything under control," Jimmy said. "I'll be the D.J." He knew how to use the equipment, and he had the CDs on Laura's song list. "I don't really like weddings *anyway*," he whispered to me.

For everyone else, it was **time to party!**

I got to sit at the bridal table. I was too far away to talk to Laura. But I sat across from Martin, Pablo's fourteen-year-old cousin, who was one of the groomsmen.

"This is the first wedding I've ever been in," Martin said. "It was so hot up there *I thought I was going to fall over.*"

"My nose itched," I said.

"Is that why you were making **chipmunk faces?**" Martin asked.

I turned red.

"I think chipmunks are **CUTE**," Martin added.

I turned redder, but I was secretly **thrilled**.

Luckily, before I could turn any redder, Uncle Jorge made a speech about Laura and Pablo.

After that, a hundred people decided to toast the bride and groom. **Not really.** It just seemed like a hundred. By the time they finished, my stomach was gurgling.

I filled my plate at the buffet. As I ate, I watched everyone.

My brother was having a blast. He played requests, and people put money in his tip jar. Letting Jimmy be the substitute D.J. had worked out perfectly.

So many things had gone wrong, but they'd turned out all right.

The wedding ceremony was beautiful. The food was fabulous. **Everyone was having fun.**

And the newlyweds looked happy when they danced as **husband and wife** for the first time.

I was happy for them, but I was kind of sad, too. Things would never be the same for Laura and me. I'd miss hanging out with her, staying up late to talk, playing cards, and crying over sappy chick flicks. **I felt like I was losing a friend.**

Cutting the Cake

Laura danced with her father. Then she danced with Pablo again, and Uncle Jorge danced with Aunt Inez.

When the song ended, Aunt Inez asked, **"Who wants cake?"**

"I do!" Joey yelled.

The guests cheered and applauded. **I whistled.**

The white wedding cake had three layers with a little bride and groom on top. Laura and Pablo stood behind the cake holding a silver cake knife.

Suddenly, I remembered another good luck custom. What if Laura and Pablo didn't know about it? I couldn't take the chance.

"Wait!" I shouted, running over.

"What is it, Claudia?" Laura asked.

"You're supposed to freeze the whole top layer," I told her. "So you can eat it on your first anniversary."

"For **good luck?**" Laura asked, smiling.

I nodded. "And there's one more thing," I said quickly. "Make sure Pablo carries you into your new house so you don't fall. It's **bad luck** if you trip."

"I'll make sure," Pablo said. "Is there anything else I should know?"

I thought hard for a second. Then I shook my head.

"No, that's it," I told them. "Freeze your cake and be really careful so that you don't trip over your threshold. **Then you won't have to worry about bridal bad luck ever again.**"

Family Tradition

After the bride and groom smushed cake in each other's mouths, Laura came over to our table. She handed me the gold bracelet.

"I want you to have this," she said.

"Why are you giving me one of your **family treasures**?" I asked.

"It's **our family treasure**. My great grandma was your great grandma too," Laura explained.

"That's right," Mom said. "Aunt Inez wore the bracelet to marry Uncle Jorge. Then she gave it to me for my wedding."

"And your mom gave it to me," Laura told me. "Now I'm giving it to you for your wedding."

"I'm not getting married," I said.

"That's what I said when your mom gave it to me. Keep it **just in case**," Laura said, smiling. "You might change your mind one day."

"Thanks," I said. I looked at the beautiful bracelet.

"Thank you for telling me about those superstitions," Laura said.

"You're not mad?" I asked, surprised.

"No!" Laura said. She laughed. "You saved me from making a ton of bad luck mistakes." She gave me **a big hug** and walked back over to Pablo.

A few minutes later, Sally told me it was time for the bouquet toss. The woman who caught the bride's flowers would be the next woman to get married.

I joined the group of women waiting to catch the flowers, but I put my hands behind my back. I wasn't taking any chances with that superstition.

Sally caught the flowers. **She was thrilled.**

After the bouquet toss, I noticed that Joey's mom looked frazzled. I decided to give her a break. I asked Joey to dance.

"No way," Joey said. He made a face. "I don't know how."

"It's easy," I said. **"And dancing is more fun than sitting."**

Jimmy played a slow song. I taught Joey the box step.

Joey watched his feet and mumbled, "Forward, over, slide, back, over, slide."

I listened to the music and daydreamed.

I was glad I didn't catch the bouquet. **Thirteen is too young to be a bride.**

But I was also glad I didn't stumble walking down the aisle. After all, maybe Laura was right. Maybe I would want to get married someday.

I'd probably have to wait until after my **seven years of bad luck** ran out, though.

CHAPTER 8

P.S.

So far, I haven't noticed any **bad luck** from breaking the mirror.

Laura called when she got back from her honeymoon. She thanked me for being a bridesmaid. She also *apologized* for not spending time with me during the wedding. Then she invited me to visit her and Pablo at their new house for **a whole weekend.**

Someday I might add getting married to my **Exciting Things To Do When I Grow Up** list. But it will be at the bottom.

About the Author

Diana G. Gallagher lives in Florida with her husband and five dogs, four cats, and a cranky parrot. Her hobbies are gardening, garage sales, and grandchildren. She has been an English equitation instructor, a professional folk musician, and an artist. However, she had aspirations to be a professional writer at the age of twelve. She has written dozens of books for kids and young adults.

About the Illustrator

Brann Garvey lives in Minneapolis, Minnesota with his wife, Keegan, their dog, Lola, and their very fat cat, Iggy. Brann graduated from Iowa State University with a bachelor of fine arts degree. He later attended the Minneapolis College of Art and Design, where he studied illustration. In his free time, Brann enjoys being with his family and friends. He brings his sketchbook everywhere he goes.

Glossary

ceremony (SER-uh-moh-nee)—formal actions, words, and music performed to mark an important occasion

honeymoon (HUHN-ee-moon)—a trip that a bride and groom take together after their wedding

party (PAR-tee)—the wedding party is the group of men and women who stand next to the bride and groom during the wedding

procession (pruh-SESH-uhn)—the people walking down the aisle

pronounce (pruh-NOUNSS)—to make a formal announcement

reception (ri-SEP-shuhn)—a formal party

rehearsal (ri-HURSS-uhl)—practice

stumble (STUHM-buhl)—to fall

superstitions (soo-pur-STI-shuhnz)—a belief that something can affect something else

symbol (SIM-buhl)—an object that represents something else

tone (TOHN)—the way something sounds

tradition (truh-DISH-uhn)—a custom that is handed down through generations

Discussion Questions

1. In this book, Claudia knows many superstitions about weddings. Do you know any superstitions? Talk about superstitions that you know.

2. Why is the title of this book *Bad Luck Bridesmaid*? What are some other titles that would work for this book?

3. Claudia feels like Laura doesn't care about her. Why? Do you think Claudia was right to feel like that? Talk about your answers.

Writing Prompts

1. Some girls like to picture their weddings day (but not Claudia!). Write about what you would like your wedding to be like if you get married.

2. Claudia has always admired her cousin Laura. Write about a family member you admire. What do you like about that person?

3. Claudia has a big family. Draw your family tree, including yourself, your siblings, your parents, your grandparents, and your great-grandparents. If you're feeling ambitious, you can add cousins, aunts, and uncles!

MORE FUN
with Claudia!

WHATEVER!

THE COMPLICATED LIFE OF

Claudia
Cristina
Cortez

BY DIANA G. GALLAGHER

BAD LUCK
BRIDESMAID

BEWARE!

THE COMPLICATED LIFE OF

Claudia
Cristina
Cortez

BY DIANA G. GALLAGHER

Claudia Cristina Cortez

Just like every other thirteen-year-old girl, Claudia Cristina Cortez has a complicated life. Whether she's studying for the big Quiz Show, babysitting her neighbor, Nick, avoiding mean Jenny Pinski, planning the seventh-grade dance, or trying desperately to pass the swimming test at camp, Claudia goes through her complicated life with confidence, cleverness, and a serious dash of cool.

David Mortimore Baxter

David is a great kid, but he has one big problem — he can't stop talking. These wildly humorous stories, told by David himself, will show readers just how much trouble a boy and his mouth can get into, whether he's going on a class trip, trying to find a missing neighbor, running a detective agency, or getting lost in the wild. David is amiable, engaging, cool, and smart enough to realize that growing up is the biggest adventure of all.

with David!

Haunted!

OF DAVID MORTIMORE BAXTER

THE SECRET LIFE OF DAVID MORTIMORE BAXTER

secrets! DAVID MORTIMORE BAXTER

BY KAREN TAYLEUR

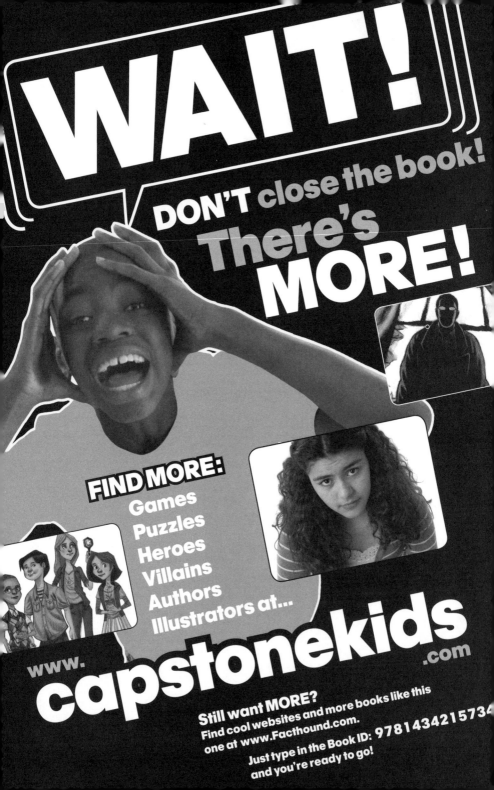